Christoph S.

Beneath the Neon lights in Tokyo

A romantic short story in Japan

Christoph S.

Beneath the Neon lights in Tokyo

A romantic short story in Japan

Impressum

Bibliografische Information der Deutschen Nationalbibliothek:
Die Deutsche Nationalbibliothek verzeichnet diese Publikation in der Deutschen Nationalbibliografie; detaillierte bibliografische Daten sind im Internet über http://dnb.dnb.de abrufbar.

Die automatisierte Analyse des Werkes, um daraus Informationen insbesondere über Muster, Trends und Korrelationen gemäß §44b UrhG („Text und Data Mining") zu gewinnen, ist untersagt.

© 2024 Christoph S.

Verlag: BoD · Books on Demand GmbH, In de Tarpen 42, 22848 Norderstedt

Druck: Libri Plureos GmbH, Friedensallee 273, 22763 Hamburg

ISBN: 978-3-7597-9375-1

Inhaltsverzeichnis

THE MEETING UNDER THE CHERRY BLOSSOMS

The city of Tokyo buzzed with life, a sprawling metropolis where tradition and modernity danced together in perfect harmony. It was early spring, and the sakura trees were in full bloom, painting the city in soft hues of pink and white. The air was crisp, filled with the scent of cherry blossoms, as locals and tourists alike flocked to parks and gardens to catch a glimpse of nature's fleeting beauty.

Amidst the sea of people in Ueno Park, Sakura Takahashi sat on a weathered wooden bench, her sketchbook resting on her lap. She had always loved this time of year—there was something magical about the way the city seemed to come alive, each petal a reminder of the beauty in transience. Sakura had been coming to this park since she was a child, and now, as an aspiring artist, it was her favorite spot to capture the essence of Tokyo.

As she sketched, her pencil gliding across the paper with practiced ease, Sakura felt a shadow fall over her. She looked up, her dark eyes meeting those of a stranger. He was tall, with a rugged, adventurous look about him—his clothes hinted at someone who had just stepped off a plane, with a leather jacket slung over his shoulder and a camera hanging around his neck.

"Sorry to bother you," the stranger said in English, his accent a mix of American and something else. "But I couldn't help noticing your drawing. Mind if I take a look?"

Sakura hesitated for a moment, then smiled. She turned the sketchbook towards him, revealing a half-finished drawing of the sakura trees, their delicate petals floating in the breeze.

"Beautiful," he murmured, crouching down to get a closer look. "You've really captured the spirit of the season."

"Thank you," Sakura replied, switching to English, her voice tinged with a hint of shyness. "I've been drawing here since I was a child."

"I can see why," he said, glancing around at the blooming trees. "This place is incredible. I'm Peter, by the way. Peter Carter."

"Sakura Takahashi," she introduced herself, a soft blush coloring her cheeks.

"What brings you to Tokyo, Peter?" Sakura asked, curious about this stranger who had appeared out of nowhere.

"A bit of everything," Peter said with a grin. "I'm a travel photographer, always on the move. But Tokyo… there's something special about this city. It's like no place I've ever been."

Sakura nodded, understanding exactly what he meant. "Tokyo has a way of drawing people in. There's always something new to discover, even for those of us who've lived here all our lives."

As they chatted, Sakura found herself drawn to Peter's easygoing nature. He was full of stories—tales of his travels around the world, the people he had met, the adventures he had experienced. There was a warmth to him, a sense of spontaneity that intrigued her.

"I've been wanting to explore the city more," Peter said after a while. "But it's always better with a local guide. Would you be up for showing me around?"

Sakura hesitated. She wasn't usually the type to go off with strangers, but there was something about Peter that made her feel at ease. Besides, the idea of seeing her city through the eyes of someone new was enticing.

"Alright," she agreed, a smile playing on her lips. "But you have to promise to teach me some photography tricks along the way."

"Deal," Peter said, his eyes lighting up with excitement. "Where should we start?"

Sakura glanced at the city skyline in the distance, thinking of all the places she loved—the hidden alleys of Asakusa, the bustling streets of Shibuya, the tranquil gardens of the Imperial Palace. There was so much to share, so much to experience.

"How about we start with the heart of the city?" she suggested. "Shibuya Crossing."

Peter grinned. "Perfect. Lead the way, Sakura."

As they walked through the park, the cherry blossoms swirling around them like confetti, Sakura couldn't help but feel that this was the beginning of something extraordinary—an adventure that would change her life in ways she had never imagined.

NEON NIGHTS

Shibuya Crossing was a dizzying kaleidoscope of movement and light, the pulse of Tokyo beating through its neon veins. The intersection was a world unto itself, where people from every corner of the globe converged, crossing paths in a fleeting, electric dance.

Sakura and Peter stood at the edge of the crossing, waiting for the light to turn green. Peter had his camera poised, capturing the vibrant chaos around them. Sakura watched him work, captivated by the way his eyes lit up with each shot he took, as if he were seeing the world through a lens of endless possibilities.

"You're really good at this," Sakura said, her voice almost lost in the noise of the city.

Peter lowered his camera and turned to her, his gaze warm and appreciative. "Thanks. But it helps to have a city like Tokyo as a subject—and someone like you to share it with."

Sakura felt her cheeks flush under his intense gaze. There was a tension between them, something unspoken yet undeniable, simmering just beneath the surface.

"Come on," Peter said, taking her hand as the lights changed and the crowd surged forward. His touch was firm yet gentle, sending a thrill up Sakura's spine.

They navigated the crossing together, weaving through the throngs of people until they reached the other side. The energy of the city was intoxicating, and Sakura felt herself being swept up in it, her usual reserve slipping away.

"Let's find somewhere quieter," Peter suggested, his voice low and inviting.

Sakura nodded, letting him lead her through the winding streets of Shibuya. They passed towering skyscrapers and hidden alleyways, the neon lights casting a soft glow on their faces. After a few minutes, Peter paused in front of a narrow staircase leading up to a rooftop bar, its entrance tucked away between two buildings.

"I know this place," Sakura said, her eyes brightening with recognition. "It has one of the best views of the city."

"Perfect," Peter replied with a smile. "Let's check it out."

They climbed the stairs together, their footsteps echoing in the narrow space. The anticipation between them grew with each step, the air thick with the promise of something more.

When they reached the rooftop, the view took Sakura's breath away. The city stretched out before them, a sea of lights twinkling against the night sky. The sounds of Tokyo were distant here, muted by the height and the gentle breeze that rustled the leaves of the rooftop garden.

They found a secluded corner with a low table and cushions, away from the few other patrons scattered around the terrace. Peter ordered drinks—two glasses of sake, the traditional rice wine smooth and warm as they sipped in silence, taking in the beauty around them.

"You were right," Peter said after a while, his voice soft. "This view is incredible. But I think I'm more interested in what's right in front of me."

Sakura looked up at him, her heart skipping a beat at the intensity in his eyes. The city seemed to fade away, leaving just the two of them in their own private world. She could feel the pull between them, magnetic and irresistible.

Without thinking, Sakura leaned closer, her lips brushing against Peter's in a tentative kiss. His response was immediate, his hand sliding into her hair as he deepened the kiss, his mouth warm and demanding against hers.

The world around them seemed to blur as their kiss grew more passionate, years of restraint melting away in the heat of the moment. Peter's hands moved to her waist, pulling her closer until she was practically in his lap. Sakura could feel the hard lines of his body against hers, the strength in his arms as they wrapped around her.

Their breaths mingled, the taste of sake lingering on their lips as the kiss became a hungry exploration of each other. Sakura's hands roamed over Peter's chest, feeling the steady thrum of his heartbeat beneath her fingertips. His touch was electrifying, igniting a fire within her that she had never felt before.

Peter's lips trailed down her neck, leaving a trail of heat in their wake. Sakura tilted her head back, her breath hitching as he found the sensitive spot just below her ear, his tongue flicking out to taste her skin. The sensation sent a shiver down her spine, and she pressed herself closer to him, craving more.

"Sakura," Peter murmured against her skin, his voice rough with desire. "You're driving me crazy."

The sound of her name on his lips, spoken with such raw need, sent a jolt of pleasure through her. She reached up, tangling her fingers in his hair as she pulled him back to her mouth, claiming his lips with a fervor that surprised even her.

Their kiss deepened, becoming a tangle of tongues and soft gasps as they explored each other with a newfound urgency. Sakura's body was on fire, every nerve ending alive with sensation as Peter's hands roamed over her, his touch both tender and possessive.

"Let's go somewhere more private," Peter whispered against her lips, his voice thick with longing.

Sakura nodded, breathless and eager. She could barely think straight, her mind clouded with desire as Peter stood, pulling her up with him. They left the rooftop bar hand in hand, the city below them a blur of lights as they made their way to Peter's nearby hotel.

The streets of Shibuya were still alive with activity as Sakura and Peter walked, hand in hand, through the neon-lit avenues. The city buzzed around them, but they were lost in their own world, the energy between them pulsing with a quiet intensity.

They paused outside a discreet entrance, a glowing red sign above it indicating a love hotel. Sakura glanced at Peter, her heart racing. There was an unspoken understanding between them, a shared desire that had been building from the moment they met.

"Are you sure?" Peter asked softly, his hand warm around hers.

Sakura nodded, her eyes meeting his with a mix of anticipation and nervous excitement. "Yes."

With that, they entered the hotel, the atmosphere shifting as the door closed behind them. The lobby was sleek and modern, with soft lighting and plush furnishings. Peter approached the reception, and after a brief exchange, they were handed a key card to one of the themed rooms.

They took the elevator up, the silence between them charged with expectation. When they reached their room, Peter slid the key card into the lock, and the door opened with a soft click. He stepped aside, allowing Sakura to enter first.

The room was beautifully designed, with a large, comfortable bed dominating the space. The walls were adorned with subtle, romantic lighting, and in one corner, a large, inviting bath filled with steaming water awaited them.

Sakura walked over to the bath, dipping her fingers into the warm water. It felt soothing, a perfect contrast to the cool night air outside. She turned to Peter, who was watching her with a look of intense admiration.

"Would you like to join me?" Sakura asked, her voice barely above a whisper.

Peter's smile was tender as he approached her, his hands gently cupping her face as he kissed her, slow and deliberate. Sakura melted into the kiss, her arms wrapping around his neck as she savored the feeling of his lips on hers.

Together, they began to undress, their movements unhurried, savoring each moment as they revealed themselves to each other. The vulnerability of being exposed, both physically and emotionally, only heightened the connection between them.

Once undressed, Peter led Sakura to the bath, helping her step in before joining her. The water enveloped them in warmth, and they settled into a comfortable silence, their bodies close as they soaked in the soothing heat.

Sakura leaned back against Peter's chest, feeling the steady rise and fall of his breath against her back. He wrapped his arms around her, holding her close as they shared this intimate moment, the outside world fading away.

"You're incredible, Sakura," Peter whispered into her ear, his voice filled with sincerity.

Sakura turned her head to look at him, her heart swelling with affection. "I've never felt this way before," she admitted, her voice trembling with emotion. "Not with anyone."

Peter's gaze softened, and he pressed a gentle kiss to her temple. "Neither have I."

They stayed in the bath for what felt like an eternity, simply enjoying each other's presence. When the water began to cool, Peter stood, offering his hand to Sakura to help her out. He wrapped a towel around her, drying her off with tender care before attending to himself.

Once dry, they moved to the bed, the sheets cool against their warmed skin. Sakura lay down, her heart pounding with anticipation as Peter joined her, his body warm and solid next to hers.

Their kisses began again, slow and explorative, building in intensity as their hands roamed over each other's bodies. Each touch, each caress, was filled with a growing passion, an unspoken promise of the night they would share.

They took their time, exploring one another with a mix of tenderness and desire, the connection between them deepening with each passing moment. It wasn't just about the physical act, but about the bond they were forging—a bond that felt as though it had been years in the making, even though they had only just met.

As they made love, their movements were a dance of mutual discovery, each bringing the other to new heights of pleasure. The room was filled with the sounds of their shared passion, their whispers and sighs mingling in the night air.

Hours passed like minutes, their bodies and souls intertwined in a beautiful rhythm. The connection they felt was more than just physical—it was emotional, spiritual, a blending of two people who had found something rare and precious in each other.

When they finally lay together, spent and sated, Sakura rested her head on Peter's chest, listening to the steady beat of his heart. His fingers traced lazy patterns on her back, a soft smile playing on his lips as he looked down at her.

"Stay with me," he whispered, his voice filled with hope.

Sakura looked up at him, her heart full. "I'm not going anywhere."

They drifted off to sleep in each other's arms, the city of Tokyo alive around them, but for now, it was just the two of them, wrapped up in a moment that neither would ever forget.

A QUIET STORM

The night air was cool against Sakura's skin as she stepped out of the love hotel. The city, still buzzing with life, felt different now—a little more intimate, a little more magical. The neon lights that had once seemed overwhelming now shimmered with a soft glow, echoing the warmth she felt inside.

Peter walked her to the curb, his hand lingering on hers as they said their goodbyes. There was a quiet understanding between them that this night, while special, was only the beginning of something more.

"Take care, Sakura," Peter said softly, his thumb brushing against her knuckles. "I'll see you tomorrow?"

Sakura nodded, a small smile playing on her lips. "I'll be looking forward to it."

With one last tender kiss, Peter flagged down a taxi for her. As she settled into the backseat, she watched him walk away, his figure blending into the bustling streets of Tokyo. The driver pulled away, and Sakura leaned back, her mind swirling with thoughts of the night they had shared.

The drive home was quiet, giving Sakura time to reflect. She had always been careful, reserved with her emotions, but Peter had stirred something deep within her—a longing she hadn't realized was there. As the taxi wound its way through the familiar streets, she wondered what tomorrow would bring and how much her life might change from this point on.

When the taxi finally pulled up to her apartment building, Sakura paid the driver and stepped out into the cool night air. The building was quiet, most of its occupants already asleep. She walked up the stairs to her floor, the sound of her footsteps echoing in the stillness.

As she unlocked the door to her apartment, a soft light greeted her from the living room. Sakura hesitated for a moment, then stepped inside, closing the door quietly behind her.

"Sakura?" a familiar voice called from the other room.

Her heart skipped a beat. It was Yuki, her stepsister. The two had been close ever since their parents had married, sharing a bond that was deep and complex. Yuki was a few years older, and there had always been an undercurrent of something more between them—something unspoken but undeniable.

"I'm home," Sakura called back, slipping off her shoes and walking into the living room.

Yuki was sitting on the couch, a book in her lap and a half-empty glass of wine on the table beside her. She looked up as Sakura entered, her eyes softening with a mix of affection and curiosity.

"You're back late," Yuki said, setting the book aside. "Had a good night?"

Sakura nodded, feeling a blush creep up her cheeks. "Yeah, it was… it was nice."

Yuki smiled, standing up and walking over to Sakura. "You're glowing," she said teasingly, her fingers brushing a strand of hair from Sakura's face. "Must have been a really nice night."

Sakura felt her breath catch at Yuki's touch, the familiar warmth between them flickering to life. She had always been close to Yuki, but recently, their relationship had started to shift, the line between family and something more becoming increasingly blurred.

"Yuki…" Sakura began, her voice faltering.

But Yuki just smiled, her eyes filled with understanding. "It's okay, Sakura. You don't have to explain anything to me."

Sakura looked up at her, feeling a swirl of emotions she couldn't quite name. Yuki had always been there for her, a constant presence in her life, and in this moment, the connection between them felt more intense than ever.

Yuki's hand lingered on Sakura's cheek, her thumb gently stroking her skin. Sakura closed her eyes, leaning into the touch, feeling the warmth and comfort that only Yuki could provide.

"You're special to me, Sakura," Yuki whispered, her voice filled with a tenderness that sent a shiver down Sakura's spine.

Sakura opened her eyes, meeting Yuki's gaze. The air between them was thick with emotion, the tension palpable. It was as if all the unspoken feelings they had harbored over the years were finally coming to the surface, demanding to be acknowledged.

Without thinking, Sakura reached up, her hand covering Yuki's as she leaned in closer. Their lips met in a soft, tentative kiss, the contact sending a jolt of electricity through Sakura's body. It was different from her kiss with Peter—deeper, more complex, filled with years of shared history and unspoken longing.

Yuki responded, her kiss growing more insistent, her arms wrapping around Sakura's waist and pulling her closer. Sakura melted into the embrace, her mind spinning as she gave in to the emotions that had been building for so long.

The kiss was slow, exploratory, each of them savoring the moment as they finally allowed themselves to express what they had kept hidden for so long. There was no rush, just the two of them, wrapped up in each other as the rest of the world faded away.

When they finally pulled back, both were breathless, their foreheads resting against each other as they tried to catch their breath. Sakura's heart was pounding in her chest, her mind a whirl of conflicting emotions.

"Yuki, I…" Sakura started, but Yuki pressed a finger to her lips, silencing her.

"Shh," Yuki whispered, her eyes filled with understanding. "We don't have to figure everything out right now. Let's just… be here, together."

Sakura nodded, grateful for Yuki's patience and care. They stood there in the quiet of the apartment, holding each other close, knowing that their relationship had changed forever. But for now, that was okay. They had time to figure things out, time to explore what this new chapter of their lives would mean.

As they finally parted and made their way to their separate rooms, Sakura's mind was filled with thoughts of both Peter and Yuki, her heart torn between the two people who meant the most to her. She knew that the road ahead wouldn't be easy, but for the first time in a long while, she felt like she was on the verge of discovering who she truly was—and what she truly wanted.

And as she lay down to sleep that night, Sakura couldn't help but wonder where this journey would take her, and how it would shape the rest of her life.

RESTLESS NIGHTS AND TEMPTING OFFERS

Peter checked into his hotel, the events of the evening playing over and over in his mind. The night with Sakura had been intense, filled with a connection that he hadn't expected to find so quickly. But now, alone in the quiet of his room, the emotions that had seemed so clear under the Tokyo sky were beginning to blur.

He tossed and turned, unable to shake the feeling that something had changed inside him. Sakura had been different — special in a way that made him wonder if he was ready for what that might mean. His life as a travel photographer had always been about moving, capturing fleeting moments and never staying in one place long enough to form attachments. But now, for the first time in a long while, he found himself questioning that lifestyle.

The glow of the city outside did little to calm his restless mind, and the hours slipped by as sleep continued to elude him. When he finally did doze off, it was fitful, filled with fragmented dreams of Sakura, of her touch, her voice, and the feeling of her body against his.

The next morning, Peter dragged himself out of bed, feeling the effects of his sleepless night weighing heavily on him. He showered and dressed, hoping the cold water would wake him up, but the fatigue clung to him like a second skin.

At work, Peter's usual sharpness was dulled, his mind wandering back to Sakura even as he tried to focus on the tasks at hand. He could tell his coworkers noticed his unusual state, but he wasn't in the mood to explain, so he simply pushed through the day, counting down the hours until he could leave.

By the time the workday ended, Peter was exhausted, but the idea of going back to his empty hotel room didn't appeal to him. He needed something to take his mind off things, something to distract him from the thoughts that had been swirling in his head since the night before.

As he was gathering his things, a couple of his coworkers approached him with easy smiles.

"Hey, Peter," one of them, a man named Hiroshi, said in a friendly tone. "You look like you could use a drink. How about joining us for some beers?"

Peter hesitated for a moment, then nodded. "Yeah, I think a drink sounds like a good idea."

The group of them headed to a nearby izakaya, a traditional Japanese pub, where the atmosphere was lively and relaxed. The small establishment was packed with salarymen unwinding after a long day, the air filled with laughter, the clink of glasses, and the aroma of grilled food.

They found a table in the corner, and soon enough, pitchers of cold beer and plates of yakitori were set before them. Peter took a long drink from his glass, the cool liquid easing some of the tension that had built up over the course of the day. The conversation flowed easily, his coworkers chatting about everything from work to sports to the latest gossip.

Peter found himself laughing along with them, the camaraderie helping to lift his spirits. It was a good distraction, and for a little while, he managed to push thoughts of Sakura to the back of his mind.

As the night wore on and the beers kept coming, Hiroshi leaned in closer to Peter, a conspiratorial grin on his face. "So, Peter," he said, his voice low enough that only Peter could hear, "you up for a bit more fun tonight?"

Peter raised an eyebrow, intrigued by the tone in Hiroshi's voice. "What do you have in mind?"

Hiroshi chuckled. "Ever been to a soapland?"

The word hung in the air between them, and Peter felt a flicker of surprise. He had heard about Tokyo's red-light districts and the infamous soaplands, but he had never been one to seek out those kinds of experiences. His life on the road had often kept him at a distance from such temptations.

"I don't know..." Peter began, but Hiroshi waved his hand dismissively.

"Come on, it's just for fun. Nothing serious. It's one of those 'when in Rome' experiences, you know? Plus, it'll help you relax after a long day."

Peter hesitated, feeling the weight of the decision. Part of him was curious, tempted by the idea of a night where he could just let go and forget everything. But another part of him—one that had grown stronger since meeting Sakura—felt uneasy about the idea.

The group was looking at him expectantly, and Peter knew he was at a crossroads. He could go along with them, embrace the experience as just another story to add to his collection, or he could walk away, stick to the path that seemed to be forming with Sakura.

Finally, he sighed and shook his head. "Thanks, Hiroshi, but I think I'm going to call it a night. I'm beat, and I've got some work to catch up on tomorrow."

Hiroshi looked disappointed but didn't push. "Alright, man, your call. Maybe next time."

Peter smiled, feeling a sense of relief as he made his excuses and left the izakaya. As he walked back to his hotel, the city's neon lights reflecting off the wet pavement, he realized just how much Sakura had already begun to influence him. He had chosen to keep himself open to whatever was building between them, rather than seeking out something empty and fleeting.

Back in his room, Peter sat by the window, looking out over the city. His thoughts drifted back to Sakura, and he wondered what she was doing, if she was thinking about him too. He knew that the road ahead with her wouldn't be easy—there were still so many questions, so much they hadn't even begun to figure out. But for now, he was content to let things unfold naturally, taking each day as it came.

As he finally climbed into bed, this time sleep came more easily, his dreams filled with the possibility of what the future might hold.

Yuki leaned against the counter of the bar where she worked, her eyes scanning the room with practiced ease. It was a typical night at the high-end hostess club in Ginza, the heart of Tokyo's mizu shōbai (water trade) district. The club was elegantly decorated, the soft lighting casting a warm glow over the polished surfaces and plush seating. The clientele was mostly wealthy businessmen, eager to unwind after long days at the office, and Yuki was one of the club's most popular hostesses.

She had always been good at this—making people feel at ease, drawing out their secrets with a smile and a few well-placed compliments. But tonight, her thoughts kept drifting back to Sakura, to the kiss they had shared, and to the complicated feelings it had stirred in her.

As she refilled a glass of whiskey for one of her regular clients, she noticed a familiar face enter the club. Hiroshi, one of Sakura's colleagues, walked in with a group of men, all of them looking a little too eager for a night of distraction.

Yuki's eyes narrowed slightly as she watched Hiroshi make his way to a table. He didn't notice her at first, too caught up in the lively conversation with his coworkers. But when he finally looked up, his eyes widened in surprise.

"Yuki? I didn't know you worked here," Hiroshi said, his tone a mix of shock and curiosity.

Yuki offered him a small, knowing smile. "There's a lot you don't know, Hiroshi."

He chuckled, but there was a hint of unease in his expression. Yuki could tell he was trying to place her, to figure out how she fit into the world he knew. She decided to make it easy for him.

"Sakura's my sister," she said casually, leaning against the table with an air of confidence.

Hiroshi's eyes widened further. "Your sister? Wow, I didn't see that coming."

Yuki smiled, but there was a sharpness to it. "No one ever does."

Hiroshi looked uncomfortable, but Yuki wasn't interested in making things easy for him. She had always been protective of Sakura, and seeing Hiroshi here, so carefree and unaware of the connection they shared, stirred something protective in her.

"Sakura mentioned you," Yuki continued, her tone light but with an undercurrent of something more. "She said you were a good coworker."

Hiroshi shifted in his seat, clearly uncertain of where the conversation was going. "Yeah, Sakura's great. We're all really fond of her."

Yuki's smile didn't reach her eyes. "I'm sure you are."

There was a brief, tense silence before Yuki straightened up and gestured for one of the other hostesses to take over the table. "Enjoy your night, Hiroshi," she said, her tone dismissive. "I've got other clients to attend to."

Hiroshi nodded, clearly relieved to be out of the conversation, and Yuki walked away, her mind already elsewhere. She needed to talk to Sakura, to figure out what was going on between her and Peter, and how Hiroshi might play into it.

Across town, Sakura was sitting at her desk, staring at her phone. She had been trying to reach Peter all day, but their schedules just didn't seem to align. Every time she called, he was either in a meeting or out of reach, and when he called back, she was caught up with her own work. It was frustrating, especially after the night they had shared.

She wanted to see him, to talk about what had happened and where they might go from here. But it seemed like the universe had other plans, throwing obstacle after obstacle in their path. Sakura sighed, leaning back in her chair. The distance between them felt like it was growing, and she hated it.

Just as she was about to try calling him again, her phone buzzed with a text message. She quickly grabbed it, hoping it was Peter, but her heart sank when she saw it was from Yuki.

We need to talk. It's important. Can you come by tonight?

Sakura frowned. Yuki was usually so casual, so lighthearted in her messages, but this one felt different—urgent. Sakura texted back quickly, agreeing.

A MISUNDERSTOOD MASSAGE

After another long and exhausting day at work, Peter felt the weight of the past few days pressing down on him. The sleepless night, the tension from trying to connect with Sakura, and the general stress of being in a foreign city had all taken their toll. As the workday came to an end, all he wanted was some relief—something to ease the knots in his back and help him relax.

He remembered passing by a sign for a massage parlor on his way to work that morning, and the idea of a soothing massage sounded perfect. After saying goodbye to his coworkers, Peter decided to head over there, hoping to unwind before the night was over.

When he reached the small, nondescript building, he saw the sign again, glowing softly in the evening light. The sign was in Japanese, but Peter recognized the kanji for "massage" and felt confident enough to give it a try. He stepped inside, greeted by the calming scent of incense and the low hum of traditional Japanese music.

The receptionist, a woman in her thirties with a warm smile, greeted him in Japanese. Though his Japanese was limited, Peter managed to communicate that he wanted a massage. The receptionist nodded and handed him a small menu with various options. He skimmed it quickly, not understanding most of the terms, but picked one that seemed reasonably priced and pointed to it.

The receptionist smiled again, nodded, and motioned for him to follow her. She led him down a narrow hallway to a dimly lit room where a masseuse was waiting. The room was small, with a soft mat on the floor and calming decor. Peter felt himself relax a bit as he took in the atmosphere. The masseuse, a petite woman with a kind face, gestured for him to lie down on the mat.

Peter complied, letting out a deep sigh as he did. The stress of the past few days seemed to melt away at the prospect of finally getting some relief.

The masseuse began her work, starting with gentle pressure on his back, moving in slow, deliberate motions. Peter closed his eyes, focusing on the sensations as his muscles began to loosen under her skilled hands. It was exactly what he needed—until he realized the massage was taking a turn he hadn't expected.

The masseuse's hands began to wander in a way that didn't feel quite professional. Peter tensed, opening his eyes in surprise. She smiled down at him, clearly mistaking his discomfort for something else.

"Relax," she said in broken English, her voice soft and soothing.

Peter's mind raced as he realized he had misunderstood the type of establishment he had walked into. What he had assumed was a regular massage parlor was clearly something different. His face flushed with embarrassment as he gently pulled away, sitting up on the mat.

"I'm sorry," Peter said, his voice strained. "I think there's been a misunderstanding."

The masseuse looked confused but nodded, stepping back to give him space. Peter quickly got to his feet, grabbing his shirt and pulling it on with a mixture of haste and awkwardness. He fumbled for his wallet, pulling out some cash and handing it to the masseuse, who accepted it with a small, uncertain smile.

"Thank you," he muttered, bowing slightly in apology before making a quick exit.

As Peter stepped out into the cool evening air, he couldn't help but laugh at himself. He had been looking for a simple way to unwind, and instead, he had walked straight into an awkward situation. Shaking his head, he decided that perhaps a quiet night back at the hotel was the better option after all.

As he made his way back through the bustling streets of Tokyo, his thoughts drifted back to Sakura. He needed to see her, to talk to her about everything that had been going on. But for tonight, he decided to take it easy—no more misunderstandings, no more surprises.

With a rueful smile, Peter made a mental note to be more careful next time he tried to navigate Tokyo's more discreet establishments. He had learned his lesson the hard way, but at least he could laugh about it now.

Yuki was on her way home after her shift at the hostess club when she noticed a familiar figure stepping out of a small building across the street. She paused, narrowing her eyes as she recognized Peter, looking slightly flustered as he hurried away from what she realized was a massage parlor—one that had a reputation for offering more than just massages.

She watched as he walked down the street, his pace quick and his expression uneasy. Yuki frowned, a mix of curiosity and concern bubbling up inside her. She knew that Peter was important to Sakura, and seeing him emerge from a place like that made her wonder what he had been up to. Yuki had always been protective of her younger sister, and this was a piece of information she couldn't keep to herself.

Later that night, after she had returned home and showered, Yuki sent a quick message to Sakura, asking if they could talk. It didn't take long for Sakura to respond, and within minutes, the two sisters were sitting in the living room, Yuki nursing a glass of wine while Sakura looked at her expectantly.

"What's up, Yuki?" Sakura asked, noticing the serious expression on her sister's face.

Yuki hesitated for a moment, not wanting to upset Sakura but knowing she had to tell her. "I saw Peter tonight," she began, keeping her tone casual but direct. "He was coming out of a massage parlor in Kabukicho."

Sakura blinked, a flicker of confusion crossing her face. "A massage parlor?"

Yuki nodded, watching Sakura's reaction closely. "Not the kind you go to for a regular massage, if you know what I mean."

There was a brief silence as Sakura processed this information. Her initial reaction was disbelief—Peter wasn't the type to seek out that kind of place. But then, doubt began to creep in. They hadn't been able to see each other much since that night, and maybe there were things about him she didn't know.

"Are you sure it was him?" Sakura asked, her voice tinged with uncertainty.

"Pretty sure," Yuki replied, taking a sip of her wine. "Look, Sakura, I'm not trying to make you worry. I just thought you should know."

Sakura nodded slowly, her mind racing. She trusted Peter, but this was unsettling. She needed time to think, to sort out her feelings. But the idea of sitting alone and stewing over it didn't appeal to her.

"I think I need a distraction," Sakura said suddenly, standing up. "There's a speed dating event tonight. Maybe I'll go. Clear my head."

Yuki raised an eyebrow but didn't argue. "If that's what you need, go for it. Just… be careful, okay?"

Sakura smiled faintly, appreciating her sister's concern. "I will. Thanks, Yuki."

A NEW PLAYER ENTERS

The speed dating event was held at a trendy café in Shibuya, with soft lighting, cozy booths, and an upbeat atmosphere. Sakura wasn't sure what to expect—she had never been to one of these events before—but the idea of meeting new people and getting her mind off Peter seemed like a good idea.

She took a deep breath as she entered the room, trying to push aside the lingering thoughts of what Yuki had told her. The room was buzzing with conversation, and she was quickly ushered to a table where the event organizer explained the rules. Each participant would have five minutes to talk with a potential match before moving on to the next person. It was quick, light, and non-committal—exactly what Sakura needed.

The first few rounds were uneventful. The men she met were polite, but none of them sparked any real interest. As she rotated to the next table, Sakura found herself sitting across from a man who looked a little different from the others. He had an intensity about him, his eyes bright behind his glasses, and he was fiddling with something under the table.

"Hi, I'm Sakura," she introduced herself, offering a polite smile.

"Sato," the man replied, his voice enthusiastic. "Nice to meet you."

There was a brief pause as Sato seemed to assess her, his eyes flicking over her with a curious intensity. "So, Sakura, do you play games?"

Sakura blinked, caught off guard by the question. "Games? You mean like video games?"

Sato nodded eagerly. "Yeah! I'm really into MMORPGs. I've been playing this new one lately, and I'm in the middle of creating a new character. I need a new female avatar, someone with a unique look and personality. I think you'd be perfect as the inspiration."

Sakura wasn't sure how to respond to that. Sato's passion for gaming was clearly deep, and while she wasn't much of a gamer herself, she couldn't help but be intrigued by his enthusiasm. "That's… interesting," she said slowly. "So you design characters based on people you meet?"

"Sometimes," Sato admitted, his eyes lighting up as he spoke. "It's all about creating someone who feels real, who has depth. I'm thinking of a character who's strong, independent, but with a mysterious side. I bet you'd make a great model for that."

Sakura smiled, a little flattered despite the oddity of the situation. "I'm not sure I'm that interesting, but thanks."

Sato leaned forward, clearly excited by the idea. "You never know! Sometimes the best characters come from the most unexpected places. If you're interested, I could show you the game sometime."

Sakura considered the offer. It was a bit out of her comfort zone, but maybe that was exactly what she needed right now — something new, something different. And Sato, with his eccentric charm, was certainly offering that.

"Maybe," she said, her smile becoming more genuine. "I'll think about it."

As the bell rang, signaling the end of their time, Sato handed Sakura his card. "If you change your mind, give me a call. We could create something amazing together."

Sakura took the card, tucking it into her purse as she moved on to the next table. She wasn't sure if she'd ever take Sato up on his offer, but the conversation had done what she needed — it had distracted her, made her think about something other than Peter and the confusion swirling around him.

As the event wound down and Sakura made her way home, she couldn't help but wonder about the paths her life was taking. There were so many questions, so many choices to make. But for now, she was content to let things unfold as they would, one day at a time.

Sato had spent the early evening engrossed in his game, meticulously designing his new female avatar while brainstorming ideas for her backstory. His excitement about the character he was creating was palpable. The in-game interactions he'd had with Yuki earlier had added a layer of inspiration—her character had been a strong, enigmatic figure that had intrigued him.

After the speed dating event, where he had met Sakura, Sato felt a compelling urge to connect with Yuki again, this time outside the virtual world. He had learned from their previous conversations that Yuki lived with her sister, Sakura, and when he mentioned to Yuki that he would be in the area, she had suggested dropping by their apartment for a casual visit.

As Sato approached the apartment building, he felt a mix of anticipation and nervousness. The building was an old, well-maintained structure, with a small lobby that exuded an old-world charm. He made his way up to the second floor, following the directions Yuki had given him.

When he reached their door, he hesitated for a moment, taking a deep breath before knocking. The door opened almost immediately, revealing Yuki standing there with a welcoming but slightly guarded smile.

"Hey, Sato," she said, stepping aside to let him in. "Come on in."

Sato stepped into the apartment, noting the contrast between the warm, lived-in feel of the space and the sleek, modern look of the game environments he was used to. The apartment had an inviting coziness, with soft lighting and comfortable furnishings.

"Thanks for having me," Sato said, looking around appreciatively.

Yuki motioned for him to sit at the dining table. "No problem. Sakura's out for a bit, so it's just us for now."

Sato nodded, taking a seat and glancing around. "I hope I'm not interrupting anything."

Yuki shook her head. "No, not at all. Sakura's been out for a while. She's got a lot on her plate lately."

As they settled into conversation, Yuki couldn't shake the feeling that there was something more beneath the surface of Sato's enthusiasm. His interest in her character and his eagerness to connect felt genuine, but she wondered about his motives. Still, she decided to put her reservations aside for now.

They talked about their favorite games, and Sato shared stories of his virtual adventures. Yuki found herself enjoying his company, despite the oddness of the situation. They laughed and joked, the atmosphere between them light and comfortable.

But as the evening wore on, a strange sense of tension began to build. Yuki couldn't shake the feeling that something was off. The conversation between them was easy, but there was an undercurrent of unease, something she couldn't quite put her finger on.

Meanwhile, Sakura was sitting in a cozy corner of a café, anxiously stirring her cup of coffee. She had decided to call Peter, hoping that they could have an honest conversation about everything that had happened lately. She needed clarity, and she hoped that meeting him face-to-face would help.

She had chosen a quiet spot, away from the hustle and bustle of the city, hoping that the serene environment would make their conversation easier. As she waited, she glanced at the door frequently, her mind racing with questions and concerns.

Just then, the bell above the café door jingled, and Peter walked in, looking as weary as she felt. He spotted Sakura and made his way over to her table, offering a tentative smile as he sat down.

"Hey," Peter said, his voice tinged with exhaustion. "Thanks for meeting me."

Sakura nodded, her expression serious. "Of course. I think we need to talk."

Peter looked at her with a mixture of curiosity and concern. "About what?"

Sakura took a deep breath, trying to find the right words. "About us. About what's been happening. Yuki saw you leaving a massage parlor last night. I don't understand what that was about."

Peter's face flushed with embarrassment, and he quickly began to explain. "I'm sorry. I didn't mean to cause any confusion. I went to what I thought was a regular massage place, but it turned out to be something else. I didn't realize it until I was already there."

Sakura listened, her expression softening slightly as she processed his explanation. "So, it was a misunderstanding?"

"Yeah," Peter confirmed, nodding. "It was an honest mistake. I was just looking for a way to relax, and I ended up in a place I didn't intend to be."

Sakura sighed, feeling a mix of relief and frustration. "I trust you, Peter. But it's been hard with everything that's been going on. I feel like there are so many misunderstandings between us."

"I know," Peter said, reaching across the table and taking her hand. "I'm sorry for any confusion or hurt. I've been trying to get in touch with you, but our schedules just haven't lined up."

Sakura squeezed his hand, appreciating the gesture. "I've been busy too. But I want us to figure things out. I don't want us to drift apart."

They sat in silence for a moment, the weight of their conversation hanging in the air. The café's soft music and the hum of conversation provided a gentle backdrop as they took in the significance of what they were discussing.

"I want that too," Peter finally said. "I want us to be clear about where we stand and what we want from each other."

Sakura nodded, her eyes meeting his with a sense of determination. "Let's take things one step at a time. We can work through this."

As they continued their conversation, Sakura felt a sense of relief. The honesty between them was a step in the right direction, and though there were still many questions to answer, she felt hopeful that they could navigate the challenges ahead.

Back at Yuki and Sakura's apartment, the mood between Sato and Yuki had shifted. The earlier lightheartedness had given way to a more contemplative atmosphere as Sato's stories about his gaming adventures seemed to hit a more personal note.

Just as Sato was about to share another anecdote, the door to the apartment opened, and Sakura stepped inside. She looked up in surprise when she saw Sato sitting at the dining table with Yuki.

"Oh, Sato," Sakura said, trying to mask her surprise. "I didn't realize you were here."

Sato stood up quickly, offering a polite bow. "Hi, Sakura. I was just visiting with Yuki. I hope I'm not interrupting."

Yuki glanced between Sakura and Sato, sensing the tension in the room. "We were just talking. How was your meeting with Peter?"

Sakura took a seat at the table, feeling a bit awkward. "It was good. We cleared up some misunderstandings."

Sato, sensing the shift in the atmosphere, decided to take his leave. "I should get going. It was nice to meet you, Sakura. And Yuki, thanks for the company."

As Sato left, the apartment felt quieter, the strange atmosphere lingering in his wake. Sakura and Yuki exchanged a glance, both feeling the weight of the evening's events.

"What did you think of Sato?" Sakura asked, trying to break the silence.

Yuki shrugged. "He's… interesting. A bit eccentric, but harmless. He seemed very focused on his gaming."

Sakura nodded, still feeling the remnants of the awkwardness from earlier. "He asked me to be a model for one of his game characters. It was flattering, but also a bit strange."

Yuki raised an eyebrow. "Sounds like he's really into his work. But it's good that you're meeting new people, I guess."

Sakura smiled faintly. "Yeah. I suppose it's a good distraction from everything else going on."

As the sisters settled into their evening routine, the complexity of their lives and relationships continued to unfold. Each new encounter and revelation seemed to add another layer to the intricate web of their lives in Tokyo. But for now, they both found solace in the simple act of being together, navigating the challenges and surprises that came their way.

Sato's evening took an unexpected turn as he found himself wandering back to the massage parlor where he had seen Peter earlier. Despite the awkward encounter with Sakura and Yuki, his curiosity about Peter and the strange connection to Yuki's sister gnawed at him. He decided to revisit the place, hoping to glean more information or simply satisfy his own intrigue.

As he entered the parlor, the familiar scent of incense and the soft murmur of ambient music greeted him. This time, he approached the receptionist with a determined air.

"Hi," Sato began, trying to sound casual. "I was here earlier today and saw someone I know. I'm curious if you might have more details about him."

The receptionist looked up from her desk, her expression neutral. "I'm sorry, but we cannot share information about our clients."

Sato nodded, understanding but still curious. "I see. I just wanted to understand what kind of place this is. It seemed a bit different from what I expected."

The receptionist's gaze softened slightly, as if recognizing Sato's genuine confusion. "We offer various services, but if you have any specific questions, I can try to help."

Sato hesitated before asking, "Do you often have people who come in by mistake, thinking it's a regular massage parlor?"

The receptionist gave a small smile. "Occasionally. Sometimes people come in looking for relaxation and find themselves in a different kind of experience."

Sato nodded thoughtfully. "I guess that's what happened to my friend."

As the conversation continued, Sato's phone buzzed with a call from Yuki. He glanced at the screen and debated answering but decided to let it go to voicemail. The atmosphere of the parlor made it difficult to talk, and he didn't want to seem rude by taking a call in the middle of his visit.

The receptionist noticed his distraction and asked, "Everything alright?"

Sato waved off the concern with a smile. "Just a call I need to deal with later. Thanks for your help."

After a brief, polite goodbye, Sato left the parlor, still pondering the strange turn of events. He decided to check his voicemail and found a message from Yuki.

"Hey Sato, it's Yuki. I tried calling you earlier. I just wanted to touch base about something important. If you get this, please call me back. Thanks!"

Sato's curiosity was piqued, and he made a mental note to call Yuki back later. For now, he decided to head home and process the day's events.

QUIET REFLECTIONS

Back at Yuki and Sakura's apartment, Sakura had settled into a quiet corner of the living room, engrossed in a graphic romantic novel about Versailles. The novel was a lush, intricate story set in the opulent world of the French court, filled with romance, intrigue, and lavish illustrations. It was a stark contrast to the complexities of her own life, offering a momentary escape into a world of grandeur and passion.

As Sakura flipped through the pages, she was captivated by the vivid descriptions and dramatic plot twists. The novel's romantic entanglements and historical setting provided a sense of relief from her own turbulent emotions. She found solace in the fictional characters' struggles and triumphs, immersing herself in their world of courtly love and scandal.

Lost in the novel's enchanting narrative, Sakura barely noticed the passage of time. The book's lush illustrations and heartfelt dialogue provided a much-needed distraction, allowing her to momentarily forget about her own worries.

When Sato finally arrived home, he checked his messages again, noting Yuki's voicemail. He decided to give her a call back, curious about what was so important.

"Hey Yuki, it's Sato," he said when she answered. "I just got your message. What's up?"

Yuki's voice came through the phone, a mix of urgency and concern. "Hi Sato. I saw you leaving the massage parlor earlier, and I've been trying to get in touch with you. I'm worried about how things are going with Sakura and Peter. There's been a lot of tension lately, and I wanted to make sure everything is okay."

Sato listened, his expression thoughtful. "I understand. I've been trying to piece together what's going on. It's a bit complicated."

Yuki sighed. "It is. Sakura and Peter have been having some misunderstandings, and I'm worried about the impact on both of them. It's been a stressful time for everyone."

Sato nodded, his thoughts drifting back to his earlier visit. "I'll do what I can to help. If there's anything specific you need from me, let me know."

"Thanks, Sato," Yuki replied, her tone appreciative. "I just wanted to keep the lines of communication open. Maybe we can all talk things through and try to clear the air."

As they ended the call, Sato felt a renewed sense of purpose. He wanted to be a positive force in this tangled situation, even if it meant navigating the complexities of relationships and misunderstandings.

Meanwhile, Sakura continued to lose herself in the world of Versailles, her thoughts drifting between the novel's dramatic love story and the real-life drama unfolding around her. She was grateful for the escape, even as she knew she would need to face the realities of her own life soon.

RESOLUTIONS AND NEW BEGIN-NINGS

47

The weeks following the tense events brought a sense of clarity and renewal for all the characters involved. Each of them began to navigate their own paths with newfound understanding and hope.

After their heartfelt café conversation, Sakura and Peter made a concerted effort to communicate more openly. They began spending more time together, addressing any lingering misunderstandings and building a stronger foundation for their relationship. Their dates became moments of genuine connection, where they talked about their hopes and dreams, their pasts and their future.

One evening, Peter surprised Sakura with a beautifully arranged picnic in a quiet Tokyo park. As they sat under a canopy of cherry blossoms, the air filled with the soft hum of the city and the gentle rustle of leaves, Peter took Sakura's hand and looked into her eyes.

"I want us to make the most of every moment we have together," Peter said softly. "I know we've had our share of challenges, but I believe in us."

Sakura smiled, feeling a deep sense of contentment. "I believe in us too. Let's continue to work on our relationship and cherish these moments."

They shared a tender kiss, the promise of a bright future reflected in their embrace. The challenges they had faced only strengthened their bond, and they both felt a renewed sense of optimism.

As for Yuki and Sato, their unexpected connection had blossomed into a genuine friendship. They continued to talk and share their interests, often discussing their favorite games and swapping stories. Yuki was pleasantly surprised by how much she enjoyed their conversations, and Sato's enthusiasm for life was infectious.

One evening, Sato invited Yuki to join him for a gaming session. As they played together, Yuki found herself getting immersed in the virtual world, enjoying the creative and interactive experience. Their playful banter and shared laughter made the gaming sessions enjoyable and light-hearted.

"I have to admit, this is a lot more fun than I expected," Yuki said with a grin.

Sato laughed. "I'm glad you're enjoying it! Maybe we can even collaborate on a game character together sometime."

Yuki's eyes sparkled with excitement. "That sounds like a great idea. Let's make it happen!"

Their friendship grew stronger with each passing day, and both Yuki and Sato found comfort and joy in their newfound connection.

The bond between Sakura and Yuki also deepened as they supported each other through the ups and downs of their lives. They spent more time together, sharing their experiences and offering each other advice and encouragement.

One weekend, they decided to take a trip to a scenic hot spring resort outside of Tokyo. The trip was a perfect opportunity for them to unwind and enjoy each other's company away from the hustle and bustle of the city. They laughed, relaxed, and talked about their futures, feeling grateful for the close bond they shared.

"I'm really glad we did this," Sakura said as they soaked in the warm, soothing waters of the hot spring.

"Me too," Yuki agreed. "It's been a challenging time, but having you by my side makes everything better."

As the steam rose from the water and the sun set in the distance, the sisters felt a deep sense of peace and contentment.

A NEW CHAPTER

With the tensions and misunderstandings behind them, Sakura, Peter, Yuki, and Sato embraced their new beginnings. Their lives, once tangled in confusion and uncertainty, now flowed with a sense of clarity and purpose.

Peter and Sakura continued to build their relationship, savoring the small moments and supporting each other's dreams. Yuki and Sato enjoyed a friendship that enriched their lives, blending their passions and creating new memories together. The bond between the sisters remained strong, providing them with a solid foundation as they faced the future.

As Tokyo's skyline shimmered under the night sky, the city seemed to reflect their newfound optimism and happiness. They had navigated the twists and turns of their individual journeys and emerged stronger and more connected than before.

With hope in their hearts and a sense of adventure ahead, Sakura, Peter, Yuki, and Sato looked forward to the future, ready to embrace whatever life had in store for them.